A NEVER-MIND BOOK

The flyaway kite

by Jane Carruth   illustrated by Tony Hutchings

Intercontinental ibp Book Productions

Hoppity always wanted to do the same things as his brother Bobtail. One day Bobtail was flying his kite. Hoppity cried, ''Let me have a try!''

He tugged the string out of Bobtail's hand. The kite flew away and landed in a tall tree.
"Now look what you have done!" said Bobtail.

Hoppity tried to climb up the tree to get the kite. But he forgot that he was wearing his new jeans. Soon he tore a big hole in them.

Back at home, Mummy and Daddy quickly found out what had happened, and they were cross with Hoppity. "What a naughty boy you are," said Daddy. "You had better go straight to bed!"

Sadly Hoppity tucked himself up in bed, and soon he
was fast asleep. Then he began to dream of kites.
Lots of brightly coloured kites, with faces, seemed
to be chasing him. Some of them seemed to be
laughing at him, others looked angry or sad.
Hoppity ran away from them as fast as he could.
"Help me! Help me!" he cried aloud.

As he woke up suddenly, he was glad
to see Mummy and Daddy standing by
the bed. Even sleepy Bobtail had
come to comfort Hoppity.
"Don't be scared," said Mummy. "We
will stay with you, and you will soon
forget your bad dream."

Hoppity soon fell asleep again, and in the morning
he felt much better. After breakfast, Bobtail set off
for school. Hoppity and his Mother waved goodbye
to him at the door.

Hoppity went back to the tree, but the kite was out of reach. "Never mind," said a little bird, "I know how we can get it down for you!"

In a minute Tim Squirrel, and many more little birds, came and rescued the kite.

"Thank you very much," called Hoppity, and he ran home with the flyaway kite under his arm.

"Look, Mummy, I've got the kite back!" he called.
But then he saw that it was torn, and had lost some
of its beautiful tail.
"Oh, dear, it's all broken," he said sadly.

Mummy had a good look at the torn kite.
"That's not so bad," she smiled, "We can make
it strong enough to fly again!"
Out came her sewing box and she sewed a neat
patch over the hole. Hoppity sat down and made
a lovely new tail to flutter behind the kite.

The day passed very quickly, and soon Bobtail came home from school. Hoppity was very glad to see his brother. "Here's your kite," he smiled. "And it's just as good as new."
Bobtail was so pleased he gave Hoppity a hug.

Hoppity had another surprise for his brother.
"Look!" he cried proudly. "Mummy mended my
torn jeans and put a patch on them, and it's just the
same shape as your kite. So now I've got a kite
of my own!"

"Perhaps we can do even better than that," said
Bobtail with a wink. He didn't tell Hoppity what
he meant, but a few days later there was a lovely
surprise for Hoppity on his birthday — a new
kite, just like Bobtail's one!
"Let's go and fly them together," cried Hoppity.
As they raced along, the little birds who had
rescued the flyaway kite joined in the fun.